Dear Readers:

Real adventure is many things—it's danger and daring and sometimes even a struggle for life or death. From competing in the Iditarod dogsled race across Alaska to sailing the Pacific Ocean, I've experienced some of this adventure myself. I try to capture this spirit in my stories, and each time I sit down to write, that challenge is a bit of an adventure in itself.

You're all a part of this adventure as well. Over the years I've had the privilege of talking with many of you in schools, and this book is the result of hearing firsthand what you want to read about most—power-packed action and excitement.

You asked for it—so hang on tight while we jump into another thrilling story in my World of Adventure.

Gary Paulsen

Gary Paulsen's World of Adventure

1. Danger on Midnight River
2. Grizzly
3. Time Benders
4. Devil's Wall
5. Skydive!
6. The Treasure Ship
7. Video Trap
8. Perfect Danger

Other books

Hatchet
Hatchet: The Return
Hatchet: Winter
Hatchet: The Call
The Voyage of the Frog
The Fourteenth Summer
Harris and Me
Nightjohn
Sarny
The Car
Canyons
Tasting the Thunder
Ice Race
Dogsong
The Schernoff Discoveries
Foxman
Soldier's Heart
My Life in Dog Years

Gary Paulsen's
World of Adventure

MACMILLAN CHILDREN'S BOOKS

First published 1996 by Bantam Doubleday Dell, USA

First published in the UK 1999 by Macmillan Children's Books
a division of Macmillan Publishers Limited
25 Eccleston Place, London SW1W 9NF
Basingstoke and Oxford

Associated companies throughout the world

ISBN 0 330 37140 1

1 3 5 7 9 8 6 4 2

A CIP catalogue record for this book is available
from the British Library

Printed and bound in Great Britain by Mackays of Chatham plc, Kent

CHAPTER 1

Thirteen-year-old Jesse Rodriguez emptied the contents of the rusty metal dustpan into the trash can and surveyed the room. Earlier the airport's small parachuting clubhouse had been full of excited students coming back from a training exercise. Now it was quiet. The only ones still here were Jesse and Buck.

Jesse smiled when he thought of Buck Sellman, the owner of the club and the small, rural airport. Buck was all right. Actually, he was more than all right. He had been airborne in the Vietnam War along with Jesse's dad. He'd lost his right leg to a land mine on the same mission during which Jesse's father had lost his life.

Buck hadn't let his disability stop him, though. When the tall, lanky ex-sergeant had been discharged, he'd bought an out-of-the-way airfield near Seattle and set up shop teaching people how to fly and skydive. To help pay the bills he'd hired a couple of other pilots and started an air freight transport company on the side.

Jesse had been coming here almost every day for the past five years, working and learning everything about parachutes and skydiving that Buck would teach him. He already knew more about rigging a chute and jumping than most of Buck's advanced students, and he lived for the day when he would be old enough to make his first jump.

The front door swung open, interrupting Jesse's thoughts. A man wearing an expensive double-breasted suit sauntered in. A pretty girl with long blond hair, who looked about the same age as Jesse, followed him. The man took off his sunglasses and inspected the lobby.

Jesse leaned the broom against the counter. "Can I help you, mister?"

The man gave him a bored look. "I doubt it. Isn't there anyone here besides"—he cleared his throat—"the janitor?"

Jesse ran his hand through his jet-black hair and

frowned. "The janitor?" Then he remembered that the dustpan was still in his other hand. "Oh, you mean me."

"Bright kid." The man sighed and took the girl's elbow. "Come on, Robin. We'll come back later, when there's someone besides the hired help around."

"Wait a minute. I'm not—"

"Is there a problem here?" Buck had been in his office and had heard the whole exchange. He winked at Jesse and then stuck his hand out toward the man. "I'm Buck Sellman, the instructor. Is there something I can do for you?"

The man reluctantly shook Buck's hand and then straightened his designer tie. "I'm J. W. Waterford the Fourth. This is my daughter, Robin. I understand that you teach skydiving here?" He didn't wait for Buck to answer. "My daughter would like to take lessons as soon as possible."

The girl glanced over at Jesse, swallowed nervously, and then tightly closed her large blue eyes.

She doesn't look like she wants lessons, Jesse thought. *I'd say she's scared stiff at the whole idea.*

Buck scratched under the collar at the back of

his orange jumpsuit. "I give lessons, and I'd be happy to teach Robin. The only problem is, according to regulations, a minor has to be sixteen before she can make her first real jump."

"I see." The man raised one eyebrow. "Perhaps you could recommend a club that would take younger members?"

Buck shook his head. "I'm afraid that's the rule at every legitimate club. But if you're still interested in joining, we can teach her everything she'll need to know to make her first jump. That way, when she's old enough, she'll practically be a professional."

Mr. Waterford folded his arms. "I don't know. . . ."

Buck smiled and showed them to the door. "Don't let me pressure you. Go home and think about it. If Robin decides to join, her age group meets on Tuesdays and Fridays at two o'clock all through the summer."

He closed the door behind the Waterfords and turned to Jesse. "Well, what did you think?"

"Why ask me?" Jesse tried not to laugh. "I'm just *the hired help.*"

"That's where you're wrong." Buck playfully punched his young friend on the shoulder. "I don't remember ever saying this job paid anything." The tall man walked down the corridor toward the practice hangar, the limp from his prosthetic leg barely noticeable. He looked over his shoulder. "Are you coming? I could sure use some help packing parachutes."

Jesse stored the broom and dustpan in a narrow closet and called after his friend, "Does this mean I'm being promoted from janitor?"

"Shut up and get in here," Buck said with a laugh.

CHAPTER 2

 "So to review: There are an endless number of ways to exit an airplane, but there is only one right way. At the jumpmaster's command, put your feet on the step. Then grasp the wing strut and pull yourself forward to a crouched position, remembering to lean well to the front. On the signal, jump backward, away from the plane, and spread out into an arch. Your body should be arched from head to toe. . . ."

Buck's voice droned on, but Jesse's attention was elsewhere. He was watching a girl with a blond ponytail approaching the edge of the training field.

Jesse moved through the small group of students to meet her. "So you decided to come after all?"

Robin shrugged. "I guess that depends on how you look at it. Let's just say it was decided for me. Sorry I'm late."

"That's okay. Buck usually takes the new people on a tour and lets them ask questions before he signs them up anyway."

Buck finished his lecture, dismissed the class, and walked over. "Hi, Robin. Glad you could make it." He looked at his watch. "Jesse, I've got an important shipment due in about now. Would you do me a favor and show Robin around the place? I'll be back just as soon as I look at the invoices."

"Sure," Jesse said. "I'll take her over to the hangar and let her check out the planes."

Robin unzipped the canvas handbag she was carrying and took out a thirty-five-millimeter camera. "Would you mind if I took some pictures? Photography is my hobby and I could get some incredible pictures here."

Jesse shrugged. "I guess not." He led the way across the field to a large arch-shaped metal building.

Robin used her zoom lens to take a picture of a small passenger plane that had just landed on the runway. She continued to snap pictures as the passengers disembarked. Two well-dressed men and a woman, all Hispanic, hurried down the steps. Through her lens Robin saw the pilot following. He was talking in a loud voice to one of the men and gesturing wildly. He looked in Robin's direction and quickly ushered the passengers inside a nearby building.

"Here's where we keep the planes the jumpers use most often," Jesse said, continuing the tour. He opened the door of the hangar, moved to the first plane, and touched the wing strut. "Buck's using this one to give a special demonstration on Saturday. If you're interested you could probably get a lot of good pictures from the landing zone."

Robin walked around the plane. "Do you ever go up? In one of these small planes, I mean?"

"Every chance I get. Buck lets me spot the jumpers and check their gear before they hop and pop. It's good experience."

"Hop and pop?" Robin looked confused.

"You know. Step out of the airplane and pull the rip cord."

"Oh." Robin snapped a picture of Jesse standing

in front of the plane. "You really like the idea of all this, don't you?"

"What? Skydiving? You bet. Someday I'm going to be the best there is." Jesse blushed. "I guess that sounds a lot like bragging."

"No. At least you know what you want. I do too." She held up the camera. "But nobody cares. My father decides what he thinks will be good for me, and right now it's conquering my fear of heights."

"You don't have anything to worry about, Robin. Buck won't take you up in a plane until you're ready."

"That'll be never in my case."

"Don't be so sure. When we get through with you, you might just change your mind and become a skydiving freak like the rest of us crazies."

"What's going on in here?" A deep, rough voice echoed across the hangar.

Jesse waited while an angry-looking young man in a pilot's jumpsuit made his way over to them.

"Nothing's going on, Pete. Buck asked me to show one of his new students around. Do you have a problem with that?"

"What's with the camera?" The man glared at Robin.

She recognized him as the pilot of the plane she had just photographed.

"It's no big deal, Pete. She just likes to take pictures." Jesse took her arm. "Come on, Robin. I'll show you the training hangar."

She followed him out the door and across a well-worn dirt trail to another building. "Who was that guy?"

"That was Peter Reeves. He's one of the pilots. I don't know what got into him. He's usually friendlier." Jesse pushed open the door and stepped inside. "This is the training hangar. Buck has done his best to simulate everything about jumping in here. See that harness?" He pointed to some webbing hanging from the high ceiling. "You can practice body position and free-fall technique while pretending to be falling through the air."

"Falling?" Robin groaned. "If you only knew how much I hate that word."

CHAPTER 3

 "Okay, Robin, when I tap your leg, arch your body and jump backward. When you hit the mattress, remember to bend your knees." Buck stood in the doorway of a make-believe wooden airplane, encouraging his new student. "That was a great landing. You're looking like a pro. Move on to the next station."

Robin stood up and stepped off the mattress. The next station was the simulated free fall. Jesse was helping a redheaded boy step out of the harness.

"You're next, Robin."

"I still don't think I'm ready for this one yet, Jesse." Robin chewed nervously on the inside of her lip and looked up at the pulley near the top of the hangar.

"Whatever you say. Pete's giving a talk on the static line over in that corner. Maybe you'd like to catch the end of it?"

Robin nodded and walked across the room. Pete seemed to have completely forgotten the incident in the hangar on Tuesday. He flashed Robin a brilliant smile and explained in detail that the static line was designed to pull the cord for first-time jumpers in case they were jittery and forgot what they were supposed to be doing.

When the lecture was over, Pete sat down in the empty chair beside her. "I want to apologize for my behavior the other day, young lady. I had just come off a long flight and was pretty short on rest. I hope there's no hard feelings."

"No problem, Mr. Reeves." Robin stood. "I understand."

"By the way, have you developed those pictures yet?"

"What?" Robin looked puzzled.

"You know. The pictures you took of the planes and the airfield. I was just wondering how they came out."

"Oh, those. No, I'm afraid I haven't gotten around to it yet."

"Well, I hope they turn out." The young pilot gave her a polite nod and moved down the corridor to the office area.

"Is he still giving you a bad time?" Jesse had seen the two talking and inched over. "If he is, all I have to do is say the word to Buck and—"

Robin shook her head. "He was apologizing. Turns out he had just finished a long flight that day and he was tired and cranky." She twisted the end of her ponytail. "Is it okay if I use the phone? I need to call the chauffeur to come and pick me up."

"Why don't you let Buck and me take you home? We're about finished up here, and besides, we have to go to town anyway to pick up some supplies."

"Are you sure?"

"I'm sure. Let's go get your stuff from the locker, and by the time we get back, Buck will be ready to leave."

Robin started down the hall. "Does everyone get this kind of special treatment here at the club? Or am I just lucky?"

13

Jesse could feel his face getting hot. He was glad it was dark in the corridor. "We try to keep all our customers happy."

Robin laughed and stepped into the locker room.

She stopped. Her locker was standing open and the contents of her canvas shoulder bag had been dumped on the floor, along with the remnants of her broken padlock.

CHAPTER 4

"Oh no! Look at my camera." Robin dropped to her knees and picked up some of the black pieces of the shattered zoom lens.

Jesse examined the locker. "Someone just busted in. Was anything taken?"

"No, I don't think so. It's just my camera—"

"Don't worry," Jesse said soothingly. "Buck will straighten it all out tomorrow. The club can take some of their dues money and buy you a new camera."

Robin sat down on the floor and stared at the pile of broken equipment. "I wonder. . . ." She opened the back of the camera.

The film was gone.

Robin's mind whirled. Only one person had been interested in her pictures—Pete Reeves.

"Jesse, I don't think this was an accident." She showed him the empty camera. "Whoever did this was after something."

"That's crazy. Who would want your film? You hardly know anybody at the club."

Robin quickly scooped the pile of broken pieces into her handbag. "I could be wrong, Jesse. But Pete was awfully interested in whether or not I had developed those pictures I took of him on the runway a couple of days ago."

Jesse rubbed his chin thoughtfully. "Now that you mention it, he did seem kind of upset about your having a camera that day."

"I have an idea." Robin grabbed his arm. "Is there any way we can check on Pete's flight schedule on Tuesday? If we knew where he went and who his passengers were, maybe we'd know why he didn't want his picture taken."

"It'll be a snap to check the logbook for his assignment. But I can tell you right now that there weren't any passengers. Pete flies transport. He doesn't carry people."

Robin stared at him. "But I saw them getting off the plane. Two men and a woman."

"Are you sure? Maybe it was a couple of flight inspectors or some of the safety crew. There are always strange people coming and going out here."

Robin shook her head. "They were passengers. I could tell by the way they were dressed. That has to be the answer. Pete was carrying some people he didn't want us to know about. So he busted up my camera and took the film to make sure we couldn't identify them."

"I don't know." Jesse paused. "That's a pretty tall accusation with no proof. If you just had those pictures . . ."

Robin folded her arms. "Who says I don't?"

CHAPTER 5

The ride into town was quiet. Buck tried several times to get a conversation started, but Jesse and Robin were both preoccupied. Buck finally gave up.

They were turning up Robin's street when Jesse broke the silence. "Buck, how well do you know Pete?"

"Not all that well, I guess. He's only been working for me about six months. But he comes highly recommended, and from what I've seen, he's a good pilot. Why do you ask?"

"Here's my stop," Robin said, and pointed to a large two-story brick house with a circular driveway. "Jesse, would you like to come in with me?

I'd really like to show you those pictures we were talking about earlier. Rodney can drive you home later."

Jesse looked at Buck for permission.

Buck shrugged. "It's okay with me. As long as you call your mom and let her know where you are."

"Thanks for the ride home, Mr. Sellman," Robin said.

"Anytime."

They waved goodbye and Robin led the way up the sidewalk to the front steps. She took out a key and opened the door. Almost like magic, a small woman in a maid's uniform appeared.

"Good afternoon, Miss Robin."

"Hi, Irma. This is my friend Jesse from the skydiving club."

The woman nodded. "May I get you or your guest anything, miss?"

"No thanks. We'll call if we change our minds." Robin waited for the maid to leave and turned to Jesse. "Like I told you before, the roll of film stolen from my camera *today* was brand new. The one from Tuesday is in my darkroom. It won't take us long to develop it. Then maybe we can see what's so important about it."

Jesse wasn't listening. Instead, he was staring at the crystal chandelier in the foyer. He took in the fountain and the marble staircase. "Wow. I've never seen anything like this before."

Robin rolled her eyes and pulled him toward the stairs. "Come on. We don't have time to stand around all day. We've got some major detective work to do."

As they climbed the stairs, Jesse tried not to gawk at the paintings along the wall. He thought he recognized famous signatures on more than one of them.

At the top of the staircase, they went through a set of double doors. Jesse, still gaping at everything, almost stepped on the back of Robin's shoe. Her bedroom was as big as his living room. The furniture was white, and framed photographs covered the walls.

He stopped in front of one. It was a large Saint Bernard with a red balloon in its mouth. "Did you take this? It's great."

"I took all of these. I'm not allowed to hang them anywhere but here"—Robin laughed—"and as you can see, I'm about out of room." She moved to a narrow door beside her dresser. "You want to help me in the darkroom or wait out here?"

"I don't know how much help I'll be, but I'll give it a try."

Robin held the door for him. "Watch your step. It's a little small. My mother had it converted from a closet."

"This used to be a closet?" Jesse shook his head in disbelief. Inside was a long work table, some plastic pans, shelves with chemicals on them, and a wire strung the length of the room with pictures clipped to it.

"Here, put these on." Robin handed him an apron and some rubber gloves.

She went to a cabinet and took out a roll of film. "This is the roll from Tuesday. Hand me that brown bottle marked 'developer,' would you?"

Jesse looked on the shelves behind him and located the bottle. He handed it to Robin. "I'll have to turn out the safelight for a few minutes while I wind the film onto a reel," she said. "Just hang on and don't move, or you might knock something over."

Jesse stood still in the pitch darkness while Robin went to work. Soon the negatives were ready and she turned the safelight back on.

Robin held the negatives up to the safelight. "Look at this. I told you there were people getting off that plane. I'll have these enlarged so that we can get a better look."

Once the film was dry, Robin moved to a machine she called an enlarger. As she worked she explained how it operated. When she was through she hung several wet pieces of photographic paper on the wire with clips.

Jesse studied the glossy, still wet photos. "Well, you're right about one thing. These people aren't part of the staff and they don't look like inspectors. But who are they?"

"The woman looks familiar." Robin held a magnifying glass up to one of the pictures. "In fact, they all do."

Chapter 6

"Jesse!" Robin burst into the training room waving a large manila envelope. "I found out who they are."

"Calm down." Jesse put his finger to his lips and whispered, "Pete's around here somewhere." In a louder voice he said, "Hi, Robin. Did you come out to get some shots of Buck's exhibition jump today?"

Robin followed his lead. "Right. That's why I'm here." She grabbed his arm and said in a low voice, "I know who those people in the picture are. Where can we talk?"

"Come on. We'll go to Buck's office. We don't have a lot of time, though. I'm going up in the plane with him in a few minutes."

"This won't take long. After you see it you might want to show it to Buck."

Footsteps sounded behind them in the hall. "Show what to Buck?"

They both whirled around. Pete Reeves was standing a few feet away.

Robin tried to act nonchalant. "Oh, it's nothing, really. I was just telling Jesse that maybe I was starting to get over my fear of heights. I thought Buck might like to know, that's all."

The pilot glanced down at the envelope. "What's in there?"

Robin took a step backward. "Nothing. Just some pictures I was going to show Jesse."

"Really? I love photography. Could I see them?" Pete reached for the envelope.

Jesse moved in front of Robin. "Maybe later, Pete. We're in a hurry right now." He took Robin's elbow and propelled her down the hall and out a side door.

"That was a close one." Robin followed him across the grass to a nearby hangar. "I guess it was a mistake to bring these pictures down here today. I was so excited, I forgot about what Pete might do."

"Well? Are you going to keep me in suspense? Who were the people in the picture?"

Robin undid the clasp on the envelope and pulled out a newspaper article. "Read this and see if you recognize anybody in the picture at the top of the page."

Jesse skimmed through the column and then looked up at the blurry newspaper photograph. "I don't believe it! These are the people in your photos. But why would Pete be transporting members of a Central American drug cartel?"

Robin pulled out another picture. "Remember the other day at my house, when I told you these people looked familiar?"

Jesse nodded.

"I couldn't shake the feeling, so I went to the library last night and did a little research. It turns out that these three had their pictures on television and in the papers about six months ago. The FBI had arranged a deal with them. In return for their cooperation in helping to capture some of their competitors, they were supposed to be given amnesty."

"I remember something about that. Didn't it backfire in some way?"

"Right. The cartel's head man, Corrubia"—Robin pointed to a portly man with a black mustache in the photograph—"planned a trap. Instead of helping the FBI catch his competitors, he *killed* them and stole all their holdings. But that's not the worst of it. The FBI team that was sent down there to make the deal was never heard from again. I'm sure Pete's getting a lot of money to fly Corrubia and his friends here."

Jesse frowned and leaned against the wall. "Robin, this is big. The authorities should hear about this."

"What do you think we should do?"

"Go home. Don't do anything until I talk to Buck. After all, it is his company. When we get back from the jump, I'll call and let you know how he wants to handle it." Jesse started for the door, then stopped. "Robin, be sure you go straight home. These people are dangerous. There's no telling what they might do to get those pictures."

"Don't worry about me." Robin put the article back inside the envelope. "I'm the fraidy-cat, remember? I won't take any chances."

"Good." Jesse moved to the door. "I'll call as soon as the plane lands. I better go. Buck's probably wondering where I am."

26

Robin tucked the envelope under her arm and stepped outside with him. She headed down a gravel path toward the back door of the main building.

There was no sign of Pete inside. At the end of a hallway, she stepped into the lobby. Through the large plate glass windows at the front of the building she could see her father's car parked by the curb.

She let out a breath. "So far so good."

When she reached the sidewalk, she started to open the car door.

Something was wrong.

Rodney always came around to open the door for her. She cupped her hands to block the sun and strained to see through the tinted windows. Someone was sitting in the front seat, all right. But it wasn't Rodney.

The driver's door opened and a tall Hispanic man jumped out and started around to her side.

Robin barely had time to think. She turned and ran for all she was worth. The man shouted something in Spanish and raced after her.

The lobby door banged shut behind her, but she knew better than to look back. If she could only find someone to help her! The hall was empty and so was the training hangar.

Robin darted out the side door of the hangar and bolted across the field. A small plane was just rolling out of a hangar, and people were standing nearby.

"Wait! Don't go!" Robin screamed.

The tall man chasing her stopped when he saw what she was doing and ducked behind a truck.

Robin was out of breath when she reached the plane. Buck took her by the shoulders. "What's wrong, Robin?"

"I . . . need . . . help." Robin gulped air and tried to collect herself.

Jesse moved to her side. "Has something happened, Robin?"

Robin nodded furiously. She was just about to explain when Pete appeared in the doorway of the small airplane. The color drained from her face and she felt dizzy.

"What's the problem out here?" Pete growled. He looked at his watch. "We're behind schedule already."

Robin swallowed. "Uh, no problem." She glanced back at the truck. "It's just that . . ."

"What is it, Robin?" Buck asked gently.

Robin swallowed again. "I've decided that I want to go up with you."

"Now that's a surprise," Buck said. "What's gotten into you?"

"Nothing. I just think it's about time for me to get over this silly thing I have about heights, that's all. Can I go?"

"Buck, we don't have time for this," Pete protested. "Your class is waiting for you at the landing zone. Let's go."

"Her dad did sign that permission slip," Jesse chimed in.

"Are you sure about this?" Buck searched her face.

"As sure as I can be." Robin tried not to look as nervous as she felt.

Buck patted her on the back. "All right. Looks like we've added a crew member."

Chapter 7

"Everything all right?" Buck asked, tapping her shoulder.

"Great!" Robin yelled over the roar of the plane's engine. She was sitting on the floor with her head down, trying not to think about where she was. It was hard, considering that the plane's door was wide open and Buck was preparing to step out on the wing strut.

Jesse adjusted the buckle on his parachute harness and stepped close to the door to watch for the landing zone. After spotting it and checking the wind indicator for the second time, he reached out and slapped Buck's thigh.

Buck's jump was perfect. He threw his body

backward into a poised arch and drifted away from the plane.

"You really ought to see this, Robin. He's the best."

Robin didn't move. "I'll take your word for it."

The rainbow-colored parachute slipped out of its deployment sleeve and blossomed in midair. Like a paper doll, Buck floated effortlessly to the ground and landed in the center of the zone.

"Right on target as usual," Jesse said proudly. He moved to the front of the plane. "You can take us in, Pete. Buck's down."

Pete nodded and turned the plane around. Jesse sat down on the floor beside Robin. Because Pete might be able to hear snatches of their conversation, he decided not to ask what had happened back at the field. Besides, Robin didn't look much like she wanted to talk right then anyway.

Jesse leaned back and closed his eyes. Someday it would be him floating down through the clouds, putting on exhibitions for students. Later he'd enter international jumping contests. When he landed perfectly on the X, the other contestants would all crowd around him begging for his autograph.

The plane lunged forward. Jesse's eyes flew

open. The engine coughed and sputtered. He jumped to his feet. "What's wrong, Pete?"

"Looks like engine failure. We're going down, kid. You and your girlfriend better get out now if you want to keep your skin." Pete unbuckled his safety belt and checked his own parachute. "What are you standing around for? Didn't you hear me? We're going to crash!"

Jesse turned to Robin. Her eyes were wide with fear. "I can't do it, Jesse!"

"Sure you can." Jesse tried to keep his voice from shaking. "It'll be just like in class. I'm going to be with you all the way. It'll be great, the biggest thrill of your life, something you can tell your grandchildren."

"I can't hold her much longer!" Pete yelled over his shoulder. "We're on fire! If we don't get out soon, it'll be too late."

Jesse helped Robin to her feet and led her to the door. "I know it's not the way you pictured your first jump, but we'll have to deal with it. Hang on to me. When it's time for you to pull your cord, I'll let go of your hand and push you away. Got it?"

"I think so."

Jesse gave her hand a squeeze. "You'll be fine.

Ready?" He looked back at the pilot. "See you on the ground, Pete."

They stepped into air.

Robin gripped Jesse's hand and closed her eyes. They were dropping fast. What was it Buck had said in class about terminal velocity? Something about how your body reached a maximum speed and then leveled out the rest of the way to the ground.

Jesse squeezed her hand again and then gently pushed her away. Robin immediately reached for the ripcord and pulled.

Nothing happened.

She felt a scream welling up in her throat. Her eyes snapped open. Jesse was a few feet away, frantically motioning for her to pull the cord.

Again and again she yanked at the cord, but the chute refused to open. She careened wildly through space.

Jesse maneuvered close to her. He grabbed for her foot but couldn't hold on to it. Her body continued to tumble helplessly end over end toward the ground.

He reached for her again, this time managing to catch his fingers on one side of her harness. She felt a slight jerk upward as his chute filled with air and lifted them both back up a few feet.

Jesse worked to help Robin to an upright position. She flung both arms around his neck and held on for dear life.

Everything on the ground started to look bigger by the second. Jesse tried to gauge when they would hit.

He suddenly realized that something was terribly wrong. Beneath them, instead of seeing the flat plains near the airfield, he saw mountains. The shapes of trees loomed below him, first small and then immense. Jesse braced for the collision.

They hit hard, crashing through dozens of layers of branches in a tall pine tree, the chute finally snagging on a thick limb.

Jesse's face was scratched and bloody. He could hardly catch his breath. His sides felt as if he'd been kicked. He looked up. The parachute was hopelessly tangled in the branches above them.

Robin's face was buried in his chest. She still had a death grip around his neck. Her hair was a mass of sticks and pine needles.

They hung there like that for a full minute. Finally Jesse found his voice. "Robin?"

"Huh?"

"Are you okay?"

Robin groaned and moved her head slightly to the left so that she could see his face. "Is the thrill over yet?"

Jesse attempted a smile, but it made his face hurt too badly. Even talking was a strain. "Almost. Now all we have to do is figure out a way to get out of this tree."

Robin glanced down. They were suspended at least twenty feet in the air. "What do jumpers usually do when this happens?"

"Believe it or not, this isn't supposed to happen. Pete must have been way off course for us to wind up here."

The limb they were hanging from suddenly made a loud cracking noise.

Jesse looked up at the growing split in the branch. "Looks like we may not have to figure a way down after—"

His words were lost in the fierce snapping of the branch. Without any further warning, the limb broke loose and they plummeted through the rest of the branches to the ground.

Chapter 8

"Jesse?" Robin touched the side of his face gingerly. His eyes were still closed. "Can you hear me?"

His lashes fluttered and then his eyes slowly opened. "I hear you." He tried to sit up but made it only to his elbows. "Man, I feel like a ton of bricks landed on me."

"Thanks a lot."

"Don't tell me it was you."

"Sorry. You did a nice job of breaking my fall, though."

"Anytime." His hand went to his forehead. A large purplish lump had already formed. It throbbed with pain when he touched it. "Ouch."

Robin gave him a sympathetic look and helped

him out of the parachute harness. "Unfortunately, you broke the tree limb's fall too—with your head."

"Great." He winced and forced himself to sit all the way up. "How long have I been out?"

"Not long. It's still early."

"Could you tell where Pete landed?"

"No." Robin picked up a small stick. "And I didn't see any sign of a plane crash either."

"He probably stayed with the plane until the last second, trying to call for help."

"Maybe." Robin drew designs in the dirt.

"Maybe? What do you mean?"

"While you were out, I had some time to think. What if Pete didn't jump at all? What if he made the whole thing up just to get us out of the plane?"

Jesse looked at her sideways. "Are you sure that limb didn't land on *your* head?"

"Think about it. What better way to get rid of two problems than to dump them out over the Cascades? If the faulty parachute didn't kill us, the trees were bound to."

"You're talking crazy. Why would Pete want to kill anybody?"

"Because he's mixed up in something too big for him and we have the proof. When I left you this morning, I went out to my dad's car. Rodney was gone. Some goon had taken his place, and he tried to grab me. That's why I ran onto the field. He was chasing me. His job was to get me, and the bad chute was meant for you."

Jesse closed his eyes. "What an idiot. I played right into Pete's hands. He probably faked the whole thing with the engine and I fell for it like a stupid sucker."

"Don't be so hard on yourself. I fell for it too. Besides, it just might work to our advantage."

"What do you mean?"

"If you can get us down out of these mountains, we'll be in a better position to spy on them than before. They might even be careless, now that they think we're out of the way."

Jesse lifted his right arm. A compass and altimeter were strapped around his sleeve. "These were my dad's. He used them in the army." Carefully he stood and took a deep breath. "I think Seattle is somewhere west of us. If we start now we should be there in a day or so."

CHAPTER 9

"What I wouldn't give for a tall glass of Irma's ice-cold lemonade."

"Cut it out, Robin. I know you're tired—we both are. But a car is bound to come along this road sometime."

"That's what you've been saying for the last hour and a half. We've been walking through trees and brush for most of the morning and so far we haven't seen anything but these old tire tracks you call a road."

"Hey, we were lucky to stumble onto these tracks. And according to my compass, they're heading in the right direction."

Robin stopped to take a pebble out of her shoe, then ran to catch up with him. "Have you thought about what we're going to do when it gets dark? They say it gets really cold in the mountains at night. Maybe we should be looking for someplace to stay."

"Where do you suggest? The Hilton?"

Robin looked at him.

"Okay, sorry. I guess we could leave the tire tracks and hike over to that hill and see what we can find."

"Wait." Robin grabbed his arm. "Did you hear that?"

Jesse listened. "Over there. It's an airplane. Maybe it's Buck." He started waving and jumping, trying to attract the pilot's attention.

"It's not Buck." Robin tried to pull him away from the road.

"How do you know?"

"Trust me, Jesse. We've got to hide."

Jesse hesitated and then bounded after her into a thick stand of trees.

The plane flew on.

When the noise of the engine had faded, Jesse stepped out of the trees. "I sure hope you know what you're doing. That plane could have been our ticket out of here."

"I know, Jesse. But what if it was Pete coming back to double-check on us? It'll be a long time before Buck or our families even know we're missing. Pete's not going to tell them he made us jump. He probably told everybody he let us off at the airfield safe and sound."

Jesse rubbed his aching forehead. "I didn't think of that. Good thing one of us is using her head." He started walking. "We better keep moving if we plan to make it back to town by tomorrow."

"I don't believe it! This really is a road. Look." Robin pointed down the tracks. "A truck."

A pair of wobbly headlights was coming over the rise just in front of them.

Jesse stepped behind a tree next to Robin. "I told you somebody would come along."

They kept back to make sure it was safe. As the rickety old pickup drew closer, they could see that the driver was an elderly man who didn't seem to be in any hurry.

"What do you think?" Jesse whispered.

Robin smiled. "I think we better hurry before we miss our ride."

They raced to the edge of the road and the truck stopped. The driver rolled the window down and stared at them as if they were ghosts. "What in Sam Hill are you two doing way up here?"

Chapter 10

"Thank you for the ride, Mr. Phillips. I know it was out of your way to bring us clear out here to the airfield." Robin slid across the seat and stepped out of the truck.

"No problem, young lady." The elderly man leaned across the seat. "But next time, you and your friend be more careful when you decide to go on a hiking trip. Those mountains can be deadly if you don't know what you're doing. You're lucky I came along."

"We'll try to be more prepared next time, Mr. Phillips." Jesse reached to shut the door. "Thanks again."

The old truck made a U-turn and headed down the road.

"Now what?" It was late afternoon. Jesse looked at the building in front of them. The only signs of people were in the lobby and on the airstrip. "Doesn't seem like there's much going on here."

"First we better call our folks so they won't send out the National Guard."

"We can use the phone in Buck's office. I have a master key. We'll use the side entrance in case Pete's still around."

When Robin had finished explaining to Irma that she would be late, she handed the receiver to Jesse. "It doesn't sound good. Irma hasn't seen Rodney or my father's car all afternoon."

Jesse quickly made his call and sat down on the edge of Buck's desk. "All set. My mom thinks I'm at your house learning about photography. I tried to call Buck, but there was no answer."

Robin stood up. "I'm worried, Jesse. What if they've done something to Rodney?"

"Maybe we should call the police?"

"Right. I'm sure they'll believe us when we explain that members of a drug cartel have kidnapped Rodney and tried to kill us."

"We have your pictures."

44

"Not anymore. I left them on the plane when we jumped."

"What about the negatives?"

"I still have those—sort of."

"Sort of?"

"I won't be able to get my hands on them for a couple of days. I was afraid someone might come looking for them so I mailed them to our beach house for safekeeping."

Jesse ran his hand through his hair. "I guess the only thing we can do now is try to find something the police will believe. Come on, we'll start with Pete's office."

CHAPTER 11

"Here's another one." Robin held her finger under an entry in the logbook. "At least we can show that Pete makes regular flights to Guatemala and the surrounding area."

Jesse closed the filing cabinet and yawned. "It's not very much, but I guess it'll have to do."

"Look at this." Robin pointed to the last entry. "He just got back from a trip down there on Thursday."

Jesse sat up. "Does it list the cargo?"

"No, just a lot of numbers."

"Let me see." He took the book from her and copied down the numbers. "All this stuff should still be stored in Hangar Three. Let's go see."

Robin quickly straightened Pete's desk and followed Jesse down the hall. "It's lucky for us that Buck trusts you with a master key."

"Speaking of Buck, I sure wish he would answer his telephone. We really need to let him in on all of this before we go to the police."

Hangar Three was more like a warehouse than an airplane hangar. Large cargo crates and cardboard boxes were stacked along the walls. A yellow forklift was sitting near the door.

Jesse flipped the lights on and showed Robin the list of cargo numbers again. "You check through the rows on that side and I'll look over here. If you find anything, yell."

Robin nodded and disappeared behind a wooden crate. Jesse moved across the room and started down the aisle between the rows of boxes.

A sound broke the stillness in the warehouse. The side door of the hangar grated open as it brushed the top of the concrete floor.

Jesse ducked behind the boxes.

He heard voices. One of them was Buck's. Jesse sighed with relief and had started to step into the aisle again when he heard Pete talking too.

"Why are the lights on in here?"

"I probably left them on when I was in here earlier." Buck limped over to the forklift and sat down on the step.

Pete looked around suspiciously. "The boys from the cartel will be here any minute. I told them you were on to us and that when you saw how much money was involved, you wanted a piece of the action."

No. Jesse's mind raced. *Not Buck. There's got to be an explanation for this. Buck's not like those creeps.*

The door scraped on the concrete a second time. From behind the boxes Jesse could see three men dressed in suits entering and carefully closing the door behind them.

Jesse recognized the leader, Corrubia, from Robin's picture. The portly man shook hands with Pete while the other two waited near the door.

"I understand you have another problem for me, Reeves? Seems as if you've been bringing me quite a few lately."

"I told you, Mr. Corrubia," Pete said, scowling. "I took care of those kids. They won't be around to bother anybody again."

"Good." The big man toyed with one end of his thick mustache. "What about him?"

Buck stood up. "I wouldn't consider me a problem if I were you, Mr. Corrubia. In fact, I'd say you and I are going to be able to help each other considerably."

"What makes you think I need your help?" Corrubia said with a sneer. "Reeves takes care of my deliveries to this area just fine."

Buck studied the man. "You need to learn to think bigger, Mr. Corrubia. Why should you be stuck with only one plane and one pilot, when you could have all of my airplanes and my whole staff at your disposal?"

Corrubia's eyes shone bright with greed. "I like the way you think, Sellman."

Jesse slumped against a box.

It moved.

"What was that?" Pete snarled. "If you've set us up, Sellman . . ."

The two men working for Corrubia rushed to the box. They dragged a struggling Jesse out into the open.

Corrubia's voice turned ugly. "I thought you said you took care of the kid."

Pete grabbed Jesse roughly by the collar. "Where's your girlfriend, kid?"

Jesse glared at him. "You ought to know, Pete. You killed her with that faulty parachute."

Pete loosened his grip. "I didn't tell her to wear it. In fact, I planned it for *you*. But like a good little Boy Scout, you brought along your own. Sounds like it worked out okay, though."

Jesse spit in Pete's face.

Pete punched the boy in the stomach and then slapped him hard, knocking him to the ground.

"That's enough, Reeves." Buck stepped forward.

"What's wrong, Sellman? Squeamish?" Pete looked down at Jesse. "This brat could land us all in jail. We can't afford to leave any witnesses lying around."

"I just don't like beating up on kids, that's all. If you're going to finish him, do it later, all at once, when you get rid of that other guy—the chauffeur."

Jesse searched Buck's face. It was hard and cold. He couldn't believe this was his friend talking.

"Once again, Mr. Sellman has a point," Corrubia said. "I suggest we move our business discussion to the plane. Reeves was going to fly us back down to my country in the morning. Why don't we all go now? I can show Mr. Sellman our operation and we can dispose of . . . shall we say"—he gave Jesse an evil smile—"our little problem, on the way."

CHAPTER 12

"The chauffeur—he is gone, Señor Corrubia." One of Corrubia's henchmen stood at the door of the plane, nervously looking at the ground.

"Gone!" Corrubia almost roared. "How could this have happened?"

"I don't understand it, sir. I tied him up myself and locked him in the trunk of the car."

Corrubia slammed his fist against the wall of the plane. "Idiots. It's amazing the police aren't already here. Reeves!" he screamed. "Get us out of here."

Buck checked his parachute and sat on one of the plane's makeshift seats beside a well-dressed woman who had been waiting for them when they came out of the hangar. "I'm starting to wonder about your operation, Corrubia. Do you always do things this sloppily?"

"Shut up, Sellman. My patience with you is already wearing thin."

The airplane rolled down the runway and slowly ascended into the sky. It was dark outside now, and the lights of the city were plainly visible below.

Jesse couldn't bring himself to look at Buck. He thought of Robin. At least she didn't have to go through another plane ride. Maybe she and Rodney could get enough evidence together to put these guys behind bars.

"This is as good a place as any!" Pete yelled from the pilot's seat. "Throw the kid out!"

Corrubia nodded at one of his men. Buck stood up. "Wait. I'll do it. I kind of owe the kid something for sneaking around behind my back."

The men looked at their boss. He nodded again. Buck grabbed Jesse by the back of his shirt and half-carried him to the door of the plane.

"Well, I guess this is goodbye, kid."

"No, Buck! Don't do—"

Jesse's words were lost in the roar of the engine as Buck pushed him out the door.

Suddenly he knew what Robin must have felt when her chute wouldn't open.

Except for one thing.

As Buck was carrying him to the door, he had clipped a safety belt around Jesse's waist. Then Buck calmly jumped out behind him.

Buck's chute slipped open gracefully and they floated quietly toward the earth.

"I *knew* you weren't in on it," Jesse said.

"Really? I could have sworn I had you going there for a minute."

"Maybe for a minute."

CHAPTER 13

Early the next morning, reporters swarmed the small airport, each trying to get a scoop on the drug cartel story.

"One more picture, Mr. Sellman. This time put the kids on your right." A photographer snapped a picture of Buck, Jesse, and Robin standing on the field in front of a small airplane.

Several reporters were asking questions at the same time. Buck pointed to a woman in a yellow suit.

"How long have you been working with the FBI on this case, Mr. Sellman?"

"Sorry. Until the case comes to court I can't answer specific questions about dates and times."

A young man stuck a microphone in Buck's face. "Were Jesse and Robin ever in any real danger?"

Buck smiled at Robin. "Not unless you call dropping two thousand feet in a free fall with no parachute real danger."

More cameras whirred and snapped and the reporters all started talking at the same time again.

Buck held up his hand. "That's all the questions for now. The FBI briefing took most of the night, and my friends and I are tired. Call tomorrow and we'll be glad to schedule you an appointment."

Buck put his arms around Jesse and Robin and firmly guided them inside the training hangar, locking the door behind them.

"Whew." Buck sat down in the nearest chair. "Those reporters are something else."

Robin pulled up the chair across from him. "I know you're tired of questions, but do you mind if we ask a couple?"

"Go ahead."

"Did you help Rodney escape?"

"No. Pete was watching me pretty closely yesterday afternoon. One of the FBI men dressed like an airport worker let him out."

"I want to know something," Jesse said. "How did you know Corrubia's plane would have to make an emergency landing a few miles from here? You had to know. The police were waiting for him."

Buck grinned mischievously. "Ever hear of a siphon hose? It seems the Feds borrowed most of Pete's fuel while he wasn't looking."

"I don't understand." Robin frowned. "Why didn't the authorities just round up Corrubia and his pals in the warehouse? Why let them take off at all?"

"Actually that was plan A. But when I found out Jesse was inside the warehouse, I got worried about his safety and went to plan B—jumping out of the plane—before they could do anything about it."

Jesse fell into one of the chairs. "So you're saying Robin and I were mostly just in the way?"

"I wouldn't go that far. You guys are going to be able to give some pretty valuable evidence—Robin's pictures, your eyewitness accounts of the deal Corrubia tried to make, and of course the threats on your lives. That alone should put them all away for a long time."

"Now I have a question for you two." Buck cocked his head. "How does it feel to be my first underage students who've made real jumps?"

Jesse leaned back in his chair. "Both of my jumps were pretty wild. I'm not sure I want to try it again real soon."

"I don't know. . . ." Robin stood and walked over to the training harness. She fingered the webbing. "I thought falling through the air like that was pretty exciting."

Buck and Jesse stared at her.

"Well, you know, once you get into it, it's kind of fun!"

GARY PAULSEN
ADVENTURE GUIDE

SKYDIVING SURVIVAL TIPS

You've joined a parachute club, spent hours in training, bought the best in modern equipment, and reached the legal age of sixteen. Now you're finally ready to make that first jump. What could possibly go wrong?

Hopefully, nothing. But to be sure you're jumping safely, remember the following:

1. Constantly check your equipment for wear and possible malfunction. You should always wear a compass (to show you the direction you're moving in) and an altimeter (to show your altitude).
2. Stay alert. Most ground obstacles can be avoided by turning downwind and running with the wind. If you're forced to land in trees, aim for the springy outer branches. If you're carried into power lines, never touch more than one line at a time.
3. If landing in water appears unavoidable, loosen the chest strap on your chute and be prepared to drop out of the harness. Since judging altitude over water is extremely difficult, don't leave your harness until you've touched the water.
4. Practice simulated emergency landings, and be prepared.

A selected list of titles available from Macmillan and Pan Books

The prices shown below are correct at the time of going to press. However, Macmillan Publishers reserve the right to show new retail prices on covers which may differ from those previously advertised.

GARY PAULSEN'S WORLD OF ADVENTURE

Danger on Midnight River	0 330 37137 1	£1.99
Grizzly	0 330 37136 3	£1.99
Time Benders	0 330 37138 X	£1.99
Devil's Wall	0 330 37139 8	£1.99
Skydive!	0 330 37140 1	£1.99
The Treasure Ship	0 330 37141 X	£1.99
Video Trap	0 330 37142 8	£1.99
Perfect Danger	0 330 37143 6	£1.99

All Macmillan titles can be ordered at your local bookshop or are available by post from:

**Book Service by Post
PO Box 29, Douglas, Isle of Man IM99 1BQ**

Credit cards accepted. For details:
Telephone: 01624 675137
Fax: 01624 670923
E-mail: bookshop@enterprise.net

Free postage and packing in the UK.
Overseas customers: add £1 per book (paperback)
and £3 per book (hardback).